Consider my jail cell, *mio compatriotta.*

Is this not the cubicle of a king?

The lodgings of a prince?

Am I, Vincenzo Peruggia,

Italian patriot without peer,

villain or victim?

Victor or vanquished?

Savior or scoundrel?

Text copyright © 2004 by J. Patrick Lewis. Illustrations copyright © 2004 by Gary Kelley

Published in 2004 by Creative Editions, 123 South Broad Street, Mankato, MN 56001 USA

Creative Editions is an imprint of The Creative Company.

Library of Congress Cataloging-in-Publication Data

Lewis, J. Patrick. The stolen smile / by J. Patrick Lewis ; illustrated by Gary Kelley.

Summary: From his jail cell in Italy, Vincenzo Peruggia tells how and why

he stole the Mona Lisa from the Louvre in 1911.

ISBN 1-56846-192-5

1. Peruggia, Vincenzo—Juvenile fiction. 2. Leonardo, da Vinci, 1452-1519. Mona Lisa—Juvenile fiction.

[1. Peruggia, Vincenzo—Fiction. 2. Leonardo, da Vinci, 1452-1519. Mona Lisa—Fiction.

3. Art thefts—Fiction.] I. Kelley, Gary, ill. II. Title.

PZ7.L5866St 2004   [Fic]—dc22   2003062742

First Edition

2 4 5 3 1

THE STOLEN SMILE

Written by J. Patrick Lewis

Illustrated by Gary Kelley

Designed by Rita Marshall

Published by Creative Editions

Mankato, Minnesota

S_i, I was sentenced to seven months in this prison gun-metal gray. A mere slap on the wrist, wouldn't you say? A trifle for the glory I have heaped upon a nation. What more proof do you need? The guards have moved me to a larger cell for I am drowning in gifts, flowers, tokens of love from my countrymen who envy my courage, whisper my name in wonder, and salute my so-called crime.

Do you see how right, how just this grand theft of mine was? The worm of agony gnawed at my heart. Leonardo da Vinci, the true Italian! Likewise his mysteriously enchanting model, the wife of Francesco del Giocondo. It drove me to the depths of delirium that his Italian *Mona Lisa* could be seen, could belong, could survive in a museum run by French lunatics!

Oh, you may think me mad, but my mission was ordained. I was to be the instrument of redemption, an honorable thief fulfilling his duty to his homeland. Let me recount for you the ingenious method of my resolve, my passion on that fateful August night in 1911 Paris.

As dusk fell, I hid in the Louvre Museum, ever alive to faith and fortune. The last lights dimmed and the door bolts slammed. Since the guard was standing watch, I gradually fell asleep in darkest shadows. It wasn't until dawn that he carelessly stepped away from his post. I tiptoed quiet as a mouse into the Salon Carré, where the treasure hung. Hush, hush....

Ah, such irony! I removed the plate of glass that covered her, the very glass that I myself, once employed at the Louvre, had put in place not ten months before. Lifting Her Magnificence oh so delicately from the frame, I stuck her in my sack, and crept out into the sunshine of history, free as a pigeon in the City of Lights. Viva Leonardo! Viva Vincenzo!

Mon Dieu! Comb the Oriental Art Gallery!

Examine the Renaissance!

Fingerprint the sculptures!

Is she hiding in Egyptian Antiquities?

What fools, these French! After my brilliantly undetectable heist, imagine how frantic that morning must have been. Listen! Can you hear those dandies shouting even now? Those *idioti* raving at the moon?

According to the newspapers, sixty investigators spyglassed to the hunt. Somewhere in Paris beyond the Right Bank of reason and the Left Bank of awe, Leonardo da Vinci's *Mona Lisa* was gone. Had she stopped smiling? Not for me. That fabulous painting had hung in the Louvre for over a century. And now, between a stunning Correggio and a beautiful Titian—there was only empty air! Four iron pegs on the wall. Eighteen pounds...of nothingness.

No sooner had they discovered the *Mona Lisa* missing than they fired the Museum director. They interviewed guards and workers, stopped boats, trains, and cars, and scratched their heads like monkeys. They found nothing, of course. I laughed when Guillaume Apollinàire, one of their poet pets, was questioned and jailed for a week. Adding farce to folly, they interrogated the young Spanish painter Pablo Picasso. No one had a clue.

Even the great Austrian writer Franz Kafka, who would have marveled at my cunning, came to stare solemnly at the space that once held the fair lady. All he saw was a bug.

For two long years I sheltered my secret in a tiny Paris garret, waiting to escape permanently. I ventured out daily to see a city in well-deserved pain. At sidewalk cafes along Montparnasse, French faces hid behind headlines.

Empty Picture Frame Discovered. Unimaginable!

Thumbprint Found But No Match Made. Outrageant!

A Scaffold Escape? Scandaleux!

The French blamed the Germans. The Germans blamed the French. The Italians blamed the Americans, who were much too busy to care. Every Frenchman had a theory; one brave Italian had the facts.

Cradling my fevered emotions, I waited, dizzy with success. Waited in secret for the world to go on spinning and to forget the *Mona Lisa* altogether. How amazingly life obliged!

In December, the Norwegian Roald Amundsen's intrepid band of mushers reached the South Pole.

In April 1912, a force of nature humbled a giant: an iceberg sliced and sunk the unsinkable *Titanic* on her maiden Atlantic voyage.

In 1913, madness goose-stepped in, and stayed. The Great War would begin a year later.

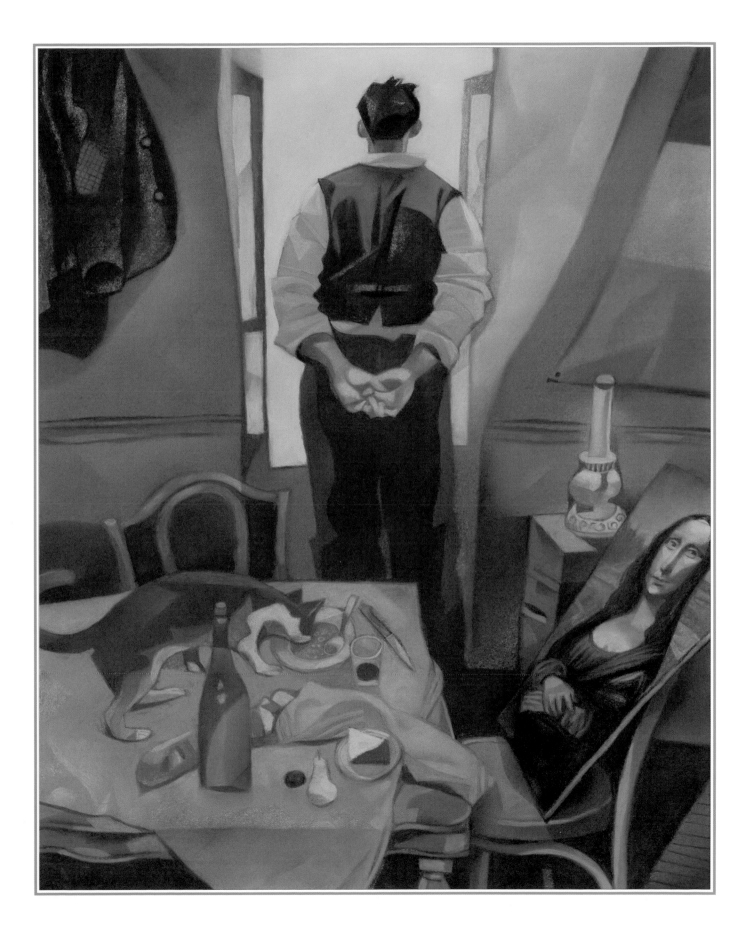

Time and circumstance—destroyers of memory—became my allies. Perhaps now an honest thief could show his hand. I took the painting and sneaked back to my beloved country, knowing that a grateful nation would welcome the gift I was about to return.

No, not a gift exactly. You must appreciate the risks I took in stealing the fair lady for Italy! The secret I kept from the world, the months of unimaginable loneliness, the toll time took on nerves as jangled as a hummingbird's and a mind as fragile as a cuckoo's.

Finally, as if it had all been precisely—deviously!—arranged, I saw an ad in a Florentine newspaper that read simply, "A buyer at good prices of art objects of every sort." Signed: Alfredo Geri, antique dealer.

Imagine Signore Geri's surprise, I thought, when I answer his ad with a letter signed by "Leonardo" himself. He will be intrigued at first, mystified—and then delighted when I offer him the *Mona Lisa* for a pittance, a mere five hundred thousand lire, or one hundred thousand dollars.

Chance smiled on me, for the antique dealer insisted on bringing the director of the Uffizi Gallery along with him. I invited them to my hotel, where I opened a wooden trunk, wildly tossing aside a shirt, underwear, a pair of worn-out shoes. *Mio dio*, what an *agitato* state I was in!

"Ecco!" I wheeled round like a swashbuckler en garde. "Our splendido masterpiece has gone missing for twenty-eight months. Home at last. She belongs to Italy, not to France!"

The museum director examined the Louvre stamps on the back of the painting and verified that it was indeed the Mona Lisa.

"Our masterpiece?" he asked. "I regret to inform you, Signore Peruggia, but four hundred years ago our great Leonardo da Vinci himself carried his own Italian painting to France and sold it to King Francis I for four thousand gold coins. The true owners of this painting are the French."

"Wait, wait, you can't do this!" I shouted as the *polizia* led me away. "*Imbecilli!* Do you mean to say Leonardo betrayed his homeland? That he had gone senile? Why else...?"

But no amount of protests would sway them. Officers of the law? These charlatans had broken trust with their own country if they could not see the justice in what I had done.

Now, as I sit behind bars, amid the aroma of flowers and misfortune, I am saddened to learn from the guards that La Gioconda, "the light-hearted woman," has since been returned to the Louvre.

Even the French call her La Joconde. Was she really light-hearted? I wile away maddening hours alone in my cell, and I wonder if, when Leonardo painted her, she had just finished writing a letter, eating dinner, playing chess, or reading a book. Sometimes, when the guards grow bored, they join me and we make a game of it, guessing what secret hides behind that face.

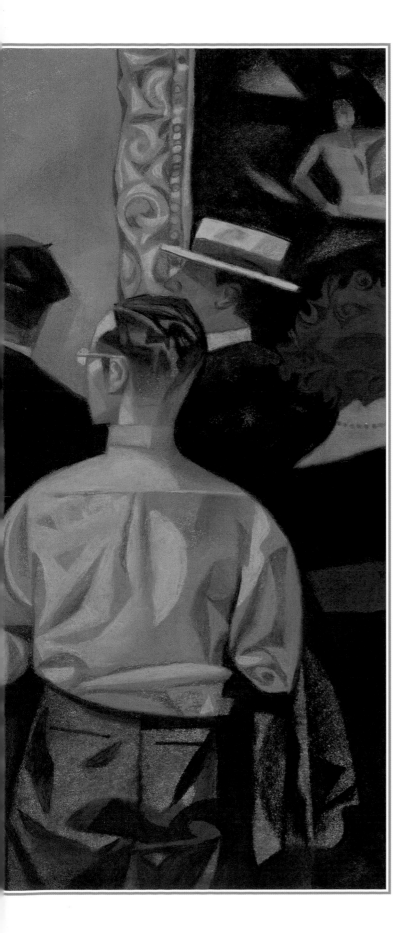

Perhaps her Museum suitors still fix her in a cool stare, as I used to do, and try very hard to look like her, to be her. But I can tell you what the world already knows: No Italian or Frenchman, no German or American has ever succeeded in imitating the Mona Lisa's smile. And no one ever will.

Although there is still some controversy as to the identity of the woman who posed for the Mona Lisa, it was almost certainly Lisa di Antonio Maria di Noldo Gherardini, the third wife of Francesco di Bartolommeo di Zanobi del Giocondo, one of the wealthiest noblemen of Florence, Italy. He commissioned Leonardo da Vinci to paint her portrait, which was begun in 1503 when Madame Gherardini was twenty-four years old.

It took Leonardo four years to complete the work, and the painting never reached its owner. Either Leonardo felt the work to be unfinished or he simply loved the painting too much to part with it. History does not tell us which.

In 1516, Leonardo went to France, where he sold the painting to King Francis I. The great lady then traveled from Fountainbleau to Paris to Versailles. After the French Revolution (1787–1793), the Louvre Museum in Paris became her new home. Emperor Napoleon Bonaparte had it removed and hung on his bedroom wall, but when he was exiled in 1815, the Mona Lisa returned to the Louvre for good. Almost.

The Louvre in Paris is one of the world's finest art museums. Established in 1793 by the French Republic, it holds vast treasures of Greek, Roman, and Egyptian antiquities. It is famous for its collection of works by Rembrandt, Rubens, Titian, and Leonardo. The Louvre's greatest sculptures include Nike, or Victory, of Samothrace and Venus of Milo.

The Italian master Antonio Allegri da Correggio (c. 1489–1534), whose paintings were influenced by Leonardo, Raphael, and Michelangelo, was one of the boldest and most inventive artists of the High Renaissance period. His *Mystical Marriage* hung on the wall to the left of the *Mona Lisa*.

✦

Like Florence and Rome, Venice was also an Italian city of artistic importance, and one of its finest artists was Tiziano Vecellio Titian (c. 1485–1576). He produced outstanding religious and portrait paintings notable for their rich colors and movement. His *Allegory of Alfonso d'Avalos* was the *Mona Lisa*'s right-hand neighbor on the Louvre wall.

✦

Guillaume Apollinàire (1880–1918) helped make the Cubist school of painting famous. He was held for one week by police investigating the *Mona Lisa* theft. The great Argentine poet and foremost Spanish-American writer Jorge Luis Borges called Apollinàire "the poet of ancient courage and ancient honor." His stature has continued to grow since his death.

✦

In widely acclaimed short stories and novels such as *The Castle* and *The Trial*, Czech-born and German-speaking Franz Kafka (1883–1924) wrote of the torment and despair of twentieth-century man. His best-known story, "The Metamorphosis," tells of Gregor Samsa, who awakes one morning to find that he has turned into a giant insect. Kafka's last wish—to have all his manuscripts destroyed upon his death— was ignored. They are now classics of modern fiction.

✦

Construction of Florence's Uffizi Gallery was begun in 1560 by the famous Medici family. It originated when Duke Cosimo de Medici I decided to create a home for the offices (hence the name "uffizi") of the Florentine State magistrates. Today, many important works of art dating from the fourteenth to eighteenth centuries are found there, including the world's largest collection of Tuscan Renaissance paintings.